Creepy
Stuff

Look for other

titles:

World's Weirdest Critters

Creepy Stuff

by Mary Packard

and the Editors of Ripley Entertainment Inc.

illustrations by Leanne Franson

SCHOLASTIC INC.

New York   Toronto   London   Auckland   Sydney
Mexico City   New Delhi   Hong Kong   Buenos Aires

Developed by Nancy Hall, Inc.
Designed by R studio T
Cover design by Atif Toor
Research by Katherine Gleason
Photo research by Laura Miller

ISBN 0-439-31457-7

12 11 10 9 8 7 6 5 4 3 2 1   1 2 3 4 5 6 / 0

Printed in the U.S.A.
First Scholastic printing, November 2001

Contents

Creepy Stuff

The Ripley Experience

A real-life "Indiana Jones," Robert Ripley traveled all over the world, tracking down amazing facts, oddities, and curiosities. A collector of just about anything and everything, Robert Ripley was never more delighted than when he happened to come across something really bizarre on one of his excursions. He was especially pleased if he could take it home with him. Shrunken heads, bone necklaces and bowls, medieval torture devices—these were the kinds of keepsakes he liked best, and they all eventually found places of honor in his home.

In keeping with Robert Ripley's fascination with the bizarre, it's not surprising that he was partial to those Believe It or Not! cartoons that dealt with the unexplainable. Robert Ripley loved a good story. If it happened to be about something ghoulish—such as the dying sculptor who carved a statue of himself, then transferred his own eyebrows, eyelashes, nails, and teeth to it—he liked it even better.

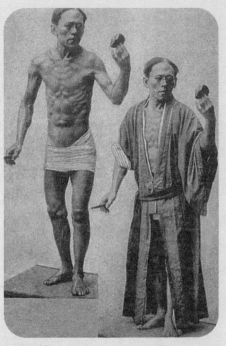

The Ripley archives are filled with tales of people suddenly waking up in morgues or sitting up in their coffins after they've been declared "dead." Whenever Robert Ripley heard stories like these, if he could verify them, he filed them away for use in future Believe It or Not! cartoons. Stories about ghosts and witches were also high up on the list of his favorite subjects.

Perhaps you've had an experience that was truly weird. Did you ever guess who was calling before you picked up the phone? Have you ever been overtaken by a feeling that felt stronger than a hunch? Can you tell when someone is staring at you before you turn around to look? If you answered "yes" to any of these questions, then you have a lot in common with the people featured in this book. Many of the ideas for Ripley's cartoons came from fans who wrote to tell him about spooky things that happened to them—about haunted houses they'd stayed in, spooky dreams that came true, or of their experiences with fortune-tellers and ESP.

You'll find all kinds of strange events in the pages of *Creepy Stuff.* You'll also get a chance to test your "stranger than fiction" smarts by answering the Believe It or Not! quizzes and Ripley Brain Buster in each chapter. Then you can take the special Pop Quiz at the end of the book and use the scorecard to find out your Ripley's Rank.

So get ready to enter a world of amazing people, places, and events—all of them unbelievable, but true.

Believe It!®

Most of us accept as truth only those things we can see, hear, touch, smell, or feel. Anything else must be science fiction. But if that's so . . .

Guesswork? In the early 1930s, Hubert Pearce guessed every card in the ESP test given by Dr. Joseph Rhine at Duke University. In fact, Pearce did just as well whether he was separated from the tester by only a screen or was in a separate building.

Believe It or Not!®

The ability to accurately predict what will happen in the future is called . . .

a. precognition.
b. X-ray vision.
c. good luck.
d. uncommon good sense.

Dead Right: In 1908, astrologer John Hazelrigg predicted that the men elected president of the United States in 1920, 1940, and 1960 would die during their terms of office—and they did.

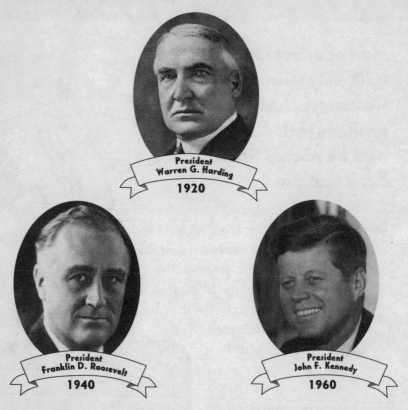

President
Warren G. Harding
1920

President
Franklin D. Roosevelt
1940

President
John F. Kennedy
1960

Bad Vibrations: In 1958, after a taxi driver was murdered in Chicago, psychic Peter Hurkos sat in the cab the driver had died in. As a result, Hurkos was able to describe the killer and provide the police with detailed information. The killer was caught.

Future Shock: In 1968, the famous astrologer Jeanne Dixon was about to give a speech at the Ambassador Hotel in Los Angeles. As she passed through the kitchen on her way to the room where she was scheduled to speak, Dixon stopped suddenly and blurted, "This is the place where Robert Kennedy

will be shot. I can see him being carried out with blood on his face." Her prediction came true on June 6, 1968.

Common Senses: Hubert Pearce, John Hazelrigg, Peter Hurkos, and Jeanne Dixon all received information in an out-of-the-ordinary way. In each case, a sense other than the usual five senses was involved. Some people refer to this extra sense as the "sixth sense," or ESP.

Believe It or Not! ®

The letters in the acronym ESP stand for the words . . .

a. extremely strange practices.
b. Earth, stars, and planets.
c. exact scientific predictions.
d. extrasensory perception.

Novel Predictions: In his 1898 novel, *Futility*, Morgan Robertson unknowingly predicted the sinking of the *Titanic* 14 years before it was built. In his story, an 800-foot ocean liner struck an iceberg on its maiden voyage one April night and sank. Even the size and capacity of the *Titanic* (3,000 passengers) matched Robertson's fictional ship, which was named the *Titan*.

Life Imitates Art:

Barzai, a book written by German novelist F.H. Gratoff in 1908, described a Japanese-American war in which unprepared American troops led by a fictional General MacArthur lost battles at first, but then rallied to defeat the Japanese. Gratoff's book was an eerie foreshadowing of actual events featuring the real General MacArthur, who led American troops to victory during World War II.

Forger's Apprentice:

The famous poet William Blake quit his job the first day that he was apprenticed to William Rylands, England's foremost engraver. Blake, who was 14 at the time, quit because when he looked at his employer, he had a chilling vision of him hanging dead on a gallows. Twelve years later, the vision came true when Rylands was hanged for forgery.

Believe It or Not!®

On the day I was born, my grandfather rode his horse around, shouting, "A United States senator has been born today!" He was right. Who was I?

a. Andrew Jackson
b. Harry S Truman
c. Lyndon B. Johnson
d. John F. Kennedy

Crystal Clear: One morning, four-year-old Crystal Guthrie, sobbing, told her mother that she had just seen her little dog killed by a truck. Anxiously, Crystal's mother went out to the backyard where she saw the puppy happily waiting for his breakfast. Minutes later, brakes screeched and a little dog cried out. Crystal's vision had come true.

Deep Reflection: In 1892, whaling captain Georges Vesperin consulted a fortune-teller in Paris, France, in a last-ditch effort to find his daughter, who had been missing for ten years. The fortune-teller said that all would be revealed in her "magic mirror." As soon as he saw the fortune-teller's mirror, Vesperin recognized it as the same one he had given to his daughter years before. Vesperin traced the mirror to a diver who had found it in the Indian Ocean while searching among the wreckage of a ship. Before long, Vesperin found his daughter living on the island of Amsterdam in the Indian Ocean.

Hot Tip: In the 1700s, well before the advent of instant media coverage, Swedish psychic Emanuel Swedenborg reported that a great fire had just broken out in Stockholm, 250 miles away. Two days later a letter reached him giving all the details of the fire—exactly as Swedenborg had described them.

Believe It or Not!®

As the most famous psychic of all time, I predicted World War II, the rise of Napoleon, the invention of the atomic bomb, and the French Revolution hundreds of years before they actually took place. My name is . . .

a. Merlin.
b. Rasputin.
c. Nostradamus.
d. Copernicus.

Picture Perfect: In 1963, psychic Irene Hughes was able to tell with uncanny accuracy what crimes each of 20 criminals had committed just by looking at their photographs.

Arresting Visions: Chris Robinson has been called "a force to be reckoned with" by Scotland Yard. Robinson is a janitor in Bedfordshire, England, by day and a psychic by night. His dream that five terrorists were planning atrocities in a hotel resulted in their arrest at that very hotel. After he had another dream that foretold an explosion at Bournemouth Pier, the police were able to locate the terrorists' bombs in time to save innocent lives.

ESP Law: Although psychic Robyn Slayden of Orlando, Florida, had no background in law, defense attorneys began calling on her in 1977 to help them select juries. Amazingly, Slayden could sense which jurors were prejudiced against defendants and predict the outcome of trials with stunning success.

Believe It or Not!®

Statistics show that more violent crimes are committed whenever . . .

a. there are high tides.
b. the moon is full.
c. it's hurricane season.
d. there's a total eclipse of the sun.

Dove Tale: In 1895, Maria Georghiu's son was kidnapped in Turkey. Seventeen years later, she dreamed that they were reunited on a journey to Cyprus. She booked passage at once. On the ship, she told a passenger about her son, describing a dove-shaped mole on his chest. The astonished man lifted his shirt to show Mrs. Georghiu the mole on his own chest. The man turned out to be her long-lost son!

Cat-astrophe: At 5:00 A.M. on November 2, 1951, Nova Churchill woke up crying, "I dreamed a black panther jumped on my mother and killed her." Later that day, Nova learned that her mother had had a heart attack while dusting a ceramic panther—at the exact moment Nova awoke.

In Plane Sight: "I could see this little girl screaming," spiritualist Francine Maness told the rescue team searching for a downed Piper Cub airplane in 1977. The searchers were then able to locate the twisted wreck in which only one member of the family had survived—a three-year-old girl.

Golden Touch: Psychic Anne Gehman can run her hands over a map and pick out places where oil will be found. She was recently shown ten potential sites and pointed to the four she was sure would be productive. Amazingly, all four turned out to be gushers.

Believe It or Not!®

Ten years ahead of time, Robert Burton (1577–1640), who wrote *The Anatomy of Melancholy*, accurately predicted the date of . . .

a. his first child's birth.
b. his own death from natural causes.
c. the onset of the bubonic plague.
d. the beginning of the Dark Ages.

Many animals can detect sounds and movements that cannot be perceived by humans . . .

Purr-fect Timing: Just before the 1925 Santa Barbara earthquake, a cat moved her newborn kittens from their home under a barn to higher ground. The quake destroyed a dam, flooding the barn.

Good Mews: Fluffy, a kitten owned by Mrs. Clyde McMillan, appeared at the office of a newspaper that had published a want ad asking for its return.

Sixth Scent: For many years, Harry Goodman's dog would walk alongside the railroad tracks with him. Then in 1968, a man was killed as he tried to cross the tracks. Afterward, the dog howled with fear whenever it approached the scene of the accident, even though it had not been present when the accident took place.

Written in the Stars: Ancient astronomers noticed the powerful effect that changes in the position of the sun and the moon had on Earth. If these heavenly bodies could influence the tides and the seasons, they reasoned, the stars and the planets could also have an effect on people.

The zodiac year is divided into 12 astrological signs, each named for a group of stars known as a constellation. According to astrologers, the sun enters a new sign each month.

Whichever sign the sun is in on the day a person is born becomes his or her astrological sign. Those who believe in astrology think that a person's astrological sign determines his or her character traits.

Taurus

Apr. 20–May 20

Gemini

May 21–June 21

Cancer

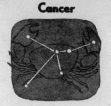

June 22–July 22

Aries

Mar. 21–Apr. 19

Pisces

Feb. 19–Mar. 20

Aquarius

Jan. 20–Feb. 18

Star-tling Acquittal: Evangeline Adams was arrested in 1914 for being a fraud. In an effort to defend herself, she asked the judge to give her the date, time of day, and place of birth of someone known only to him. With this information, Adams drew up an astrological chart that described the person to a T. The judge was so impressed that he dismissed the case, and Adams was cleared of all charges. Whom had she described so well? None other than the judge's own son!

Astro-nomical Mistake: An astrologer warned Catherine de Médicis (1519–1589), queen of France, to "beware of St. Germain." Since her palace was in the St. Germain district of Paris, the Queen moved to another area at once. Not long afterward, she felt sick and had a priest called. That very evening she died unexpectedly. The name of the priest? Jullien de St. Germain.

Leo

July 23–Aug. 22

Virgo

Aug. 23–Sept. 22

Libra

Sept. 23–Oct. 23

Star Link: King George III and an ironworker named Samuel Hemming were both born in the same town at the  same moment on June 4, 1738. These astrological time-twins both married on September 8, 1761. Each had nine sons and six daughters. Both fell ill at exactly the same time and died on January 29, 1820. Was it a coincidence—or were their lives linked by the stars? What do you think?

Scorpio

Oct. 24–Nov. 21

Sagittarius

Nov. 22–Dec. 21

Capricorn

Dec. 22–Jan. 19

Believe It or Not!®

In what country do engaged couples usually have their horoscopes charted to set the wedding date and to find out whether their marriage is likely to succeed?

a. In Norway.
b. In Greece.
c. In India.
d. In Israel.

Star-crossed: One March night, Julius Caesar's wife dreamed that a statue of her husband was dripping with blood. The next morning, she warned him not to go to the senate, but he refused to listen. That day, March 15, Julius Caesar was stabbed to death by senators who feared he was becoming too powerful.

Serious Shell Shock: The ancient Greek playwright Aeschylus (525–426 B.C.) never went outdoors during storms because an astrologer had warned him that he would die by a blow from the heavens. One sunny day, Aeschylus was sitting outside when an eagle mistook his bald head for a rock. It dropped a huge tortoise on him to break its shell— and killed Aeschylus.

Believe It or Not!®

In New England, a prediction inserted into *The Old Farmer's Almanac* as a prank came true in July 1816 when . . .

a. it rained for 30 days.
b. it snowed three times.
c. there were three solar eclipses.
d. the temperature topped 100 degrees 14 days in a row.

The time has come to test your knowledge of the eerily bizarre, the inexplicably spooky, and the unbelievably strange!

The Ripley files are packed with info that's too out-there to believe. Each shocking oddity proves that truth is stranger than fiction. But it takes a keen eye, a sharp mind, and good instincts to spot the difference. Are you up for the challenge?

Each Ripley's Brain Buster contains groups of four unbelievable oddities. In each group of oddities only **one** is **false.** Read each extraordinary entry and circle whether you **Believe It!** or **Not!** And if you think you can handle it, take on the bonus question in each section. Then, flip to the end of the book where you'll find a place to keep track of your score and rate your skills.

Which is stranger, fact or fiction? Here is your first chilling challenge. Can you sense which one of the four strange tales below is 100% invented?

a. After pulling an "all-nighter" to study for a final exam in pre-calculus, 16-year-old Anika Storm dreamed that she was successfully solving math problems in her sleep. Anika was overjoyed during her exam the next day when she realized she had worked out most of the problems the night before—in her dreams!

Believe It!   **Not!**

b. In the 1930s, astrologer Evangeline Adams charted the horoscope of the United States. Since it was born on July 4, its sign is Cancer. According to its horoscope, it's a restless, inventive country with a great deal of talent.

Believe It!   **Not!**

c. Before an earthquake hit the French Riviera in 1887, horses all over the area refused to eat and tried to break out of their stalls.

Believe It!   **Not!**

d. Halley's comet can be seen from Earth only once every 75 years. When Samuel Langhorne Clemens, also known as Mark Twain, was born in 1835, the comet could be seen in the sky. Twain predicted that just as he had come in with the comet, he would go out with it. In April 1910, the comet returned, and on April 21, 1910, Mark Twain passed away.

Believe It!   **Not!**

● ●

BONUS QUESTION

John Dee invented the crystal ball in the mid-1500s. What was his occupation?

a. He was a fortune-teller in Granada, Spain.

b. He was a renowned glass blower and shopkeeper in Paris, France.

c. He was a mathematician and president of Manchester College in England.

When two or more remarkable things happen at the same time, most of us chalk it up to coincidence. But some stories are so amazing it's hard to believe fate might not also be at work.

Same Time, Next Year:

Brothers Neville and Erskine L. Ebbin of Bermuda died one year apart after being struck by the same taxi that was being driven by the same driver and carrying the same passenger.

Believe It or Not!®

In the heat of battle, Patrick Ferguson had the chance to shoot a man in the back, but his sense of honor would not allow him to. The name of the man Ferguson spared was . . .

a. Theodore Roosevelt.
b. Thomas Jefferson.
c. Dwight D. Eisenhower.
d. George Washington.

Coat of Doom: Jabez Spicer of Leyden, Massachusetts, was killed by two bullets on January 25, 1787, in Shays' Rebellion at Springfield Arsenal. Jabez was wearing the coat his brother Daniel had been wearing when he was killed by two bullets on March 5, 1784. The bullets that killed Jabez passed through the same two holes that had been made when Daniel was killed three years earlier.

Pocket Protector:
Detective Melvin Lobbet of Buffalo, New York, was shot by a .38 caliber revolver at close range. He was saved when the bullet hit his badge— which he had dropped into his coat pocket only a moment before.

Believe It or Not!®

Angel Santana of New York City escaped unharmed when a robber's bullet bounced off his . . .

a. pants zipper.
b. shatterproof sunglasses.
c. wedding band.
d. right biceps.

Shattering Talent: In the 1800s, Etienne Laine, a vegetable peddler who lived in Paris, France, came to the attention of the director of the Royal Academy of Music when his shouts of "Buy my asparagus" shattered a window in the director's office. The director was so impressed he made Laine a star tenor in the Paris opera.

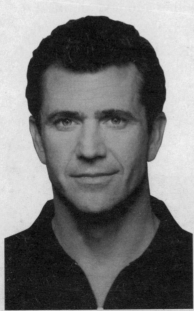

Mugging for the Camera: Mel Gibson was mugged the night before his first screen test. It's a good thing he decided to go anyway because when he got there, he found out that the role called for someone who looked weary, beaten up, and scared. He got the part— the starring role in *Mad Max*.

Mc-Multiples: George McDaniels and his entire family—father, mother, sister, two brothers, and an uncle—were all born on the same day of the year.

Statistical Leap:
Elizabeth Elchlinger of Parma, Ohio, and her son Michael were both born on February 29, which comes only once every four years. The odds of a mother and son being born on that date are over two million to one.

Rekindled Kin: Different families adopted identical twins Mark Newman and Jerry Levey five days after they were born. Both twins grew up to be firefighters, and in 1954, they found each other entirely by chance at a firefighters' convention.

Parallel Lives: The "Jim" twins were separated at birth and raised apart. Yet a 1979 study revealed that both brothers married women named Linda, then divorced and married women named Betty. One brother named his first son James Alan and the other named his James Allen. Both brothers named their dog Toy and drove the same make of car. Both did well in math, liked woodworking, and suffered from frequent headaches.

Branded at Birth: In 1901, the Meudelle twins were born in Paris, France. Each child had a birthmark on one shoulder that formed the initials of the maternal grandparent after whom the twin was named. The boy bore the letters T R and was named for his grandfather, Theodore Rodolphe. His sister bore the letters B V and was named for her grandmother, Berthe Violette.

Believe It or Not!®

The astrological sign for June is twins. This sign is called . . .

a. Gemini.
b. Sagittarius.
c. Taurus.
d. Libra.

Ate His Fish and His Words: Moses Carlton, a wealthy shipping magnate from Wiscasset, Maine, threw his gold ring into the Sheepscot River and boasted, "There is as much chance of my dying a poor man as there is of ever finding that ring again." A few days later, Carlton found the ring in a fish served to him in a restaurant. Soon after, President Madison placed an embargo on American ships, causing Carlton to lose his fortune, and sure enough, he died a poor man.

Died Laughing: Although apparently in good health, English dramatist Edward Moore sent his own obituary to the newspapers as a joke, giving the next day as his date of death. Moore suddenly became ill and died—the next day!

Disarmed: The sixth Viscount of Strathallan on the Isle of Mulligan, Scotland, swore he would give his good right arm to win a lawsuit. He won the case. A month later, he was inspecting a factory when a flywheel cut off his right arm below the elbow.

Unlucky Streaks:

Lightning struck the house of R. Scott Andres of Virgin Arm, Newfoundland, Canada, on July 4, 1985. The very next night, his sister's house in North Bay, Ontario, was also struck by lightning.

Believe It or Not!®

When his soldiers complained about being stationed overseas, an army captain responded by saying, "I'd rather be here than be president of the United States." The name of this future president was . . .

a. John F. Kennedy.
b. Harry S Truman.
c. Dwight D. Eisenhower.
d. Andrew Jackson.

Venetian Bind: Francesco delle Barche, who lived in Venice during the 14th century, invented a catapult that could hurl a 3,000-pound missile. Unfortunately, he became entangled in it during a battle and was hurtled into the center of the town. His body struck his own wife, and both were killed instantly.

Deeply Troubling: In 1988, Wright Skinner, Jr., fell into Winyah Bay in Georgetown, South Carolina, on February 13, becoming the fifth person lost in its murky depths on the same date within 11 years.

Common Scents: A traveler standing in a railway station in Stillwater, Oklahoma, was eating an apple when a stranger approached and said, "That smells like a North Carolina apple." The traveler replied, "It is. I'm from North Carolina." "So am I," said the stranger. It turned out that the two men were brothers who had not met in 30 years.

Scat, Cat—or Not? If a black cat ran across your path in the United States, you might expect to be in for some bad luck. In England, on the other hand, a black cat crossing your path means you can expect good fortune, and a white cat signifies bad luck.

Believe It or Not!®

Triskaidekaphobia is so widespread that 90 percent of the high-rise buildings in the United States have no . . .

a. 13th floor.
b. mirrors in the lobbies.
c. pictures of black cats.
d. cracks on the floors.

Two of America's most beloved presidents are linked by an eerie set of coincidences . . .

✦ Both John F. Kennedy and Abraham Lincoln were deeply involved in the civil rights issue of his era. In Lincoln's time, the issue was slavery; in Kennedy's time, it was segregation.

✦ Both were assassinated.

✦ Lincoln's assassin, John Wilkes Booth, was born in 1839. Kennedy's assassin, Lee Harvey Oswald, was born in 1939.

✦ Lincoln had a secretary named Kennedy who warned him not to go to the theater the night he died. Kennedy had a secretary named Lincoln who warned him not to go to Dallas.

✦ Both were shot on a Friday.

✦ Each wife was present when her husband was shot.

✦ Booth shot Lincoln in a theater and ran into a warehouse. Oswald shot Kennedy from a warehouse and ran into a theater.

✦ Both were succeeded by men named Johnson.

✦ Both Johnsons were Democrats from the South.

✦ The Johnson who succeeded Lincoln was born in 1808. The Johnson who succeeded Kennedy was born in 1908.

✦ Both presidents' last names have seven letters; their successors' first and last names combined have 13 letters; and their assassins' first and last names combined have 15 letters.

Believe It or Not!®

In 1872, Baron Roemire de Tarazone of France was murdered by an assassin named Claude Volbonne. Twenty-one years later, his son was murdered . . .

a. on the very same street.
b. by the son of Claude Volbonne.
c. by another Claude Volbonne who was unrelated to his father's murderer.
d. on the exact same date.

Holy Smoke Screen:

The 14th Dalai Lama of Tibet was held prisoner of the Communist Chinese in his own palace. He planned his escape on the afternoon of March 17, 1959. Although Chinese troops surrounded the palace and huge searchlights were trained on the building, the Dalai Lama and 80 companions escaped under cover of a sudden sandstorm.

Hugh Who? In 1664, 1785, and 1820, three unrelated men, all named Hugh Williams, were the sole survivors of three different disasters at sea.

Believe It or Not!®

The laws of chance are not enough to explain the large number of ships and aircraft that have disappeared in an area of the Atlantic Ocean called the . . .

a. Bahamas Quadrangle.
b. Bermuda Triangle.
c. Granada Square.
d. Colombia Circle.

Below are four creepy coincidences that will challenge your ability to tell fact from fiction. Only one of these eerie tales is false. Can you tell which one? Take a chance!

a. In Howe, Indiana, the "Animal Woman" lived with skunks and did not bathe or change her clothes for 25 years. When she was finally given a bath, she died ten days later!

Believe It!   **Not!**

b. In 1965, Anna Moses of Pittsburgh, Pennsylvania, comforted an older woman who was crying in a neighborhood park. She bought the woman a cup of tea, and sat with her until she had calmed down. Thirty years later, Anna received a letter from a lawyer alerting her that the older woman—who had inherited a large fortune after the death of a beloved aunt—had recently passed away and left Anna $500,000 in gratitude for her kindness.

Believe It!   **Not!**

c. Stephen Law of Markham, Ontario, was searching for a ring that his father had lost in five feet of lake water. He didn't find his father's ring, but he stumbled upon a topaz ring his grandmother had lost 41 years earlier in the same lake!

Believe It!   **Not!**

d. A bank customer who tried to cash a check in Monroe Township, New Jersey, was arrested when the teller turned out to be the Linda Brandimato to whom the check was made out.

Believe It!   **Not!**

• •

BONUS QUESTION

Some might say the marriage of Mr. and Mrs. Joseph Meyerberg of Brooklyn, New York, was "meant to be." What did they discover after their wedding?

a. That their great-grandparents came from the same small town in Germany and were childhood sweethearts.

b. That her Social Security number was 064-01-8089, and his Social Security number was 064-01-8090.

c. That they both attended kindergarten at the same school in Germany and were best friends before their families immigrated to Brooklyn.

Most of us would scoff at the idea that unknown forces could possess an inanimate object, but then again . . .

Hope Against Hope: Bad luck has followed the Hope Diamond ever since a jeweler brought it from India to France in the 17th century. The jeweler was killed by a pack of mad dogs. In 1793, owners Louis XVI and Marie Antoinette were beheaded. After American socialite Evalyn Walsh McLean bought the diamond in 1911, her son was killed in a car accident, her daughter died of an overdose, and her husband died in a mental hospital. Today, the blue 45.52-carat Hope Diamond is in the Smithsonian, which, so far at least, remains intact.

Believe It or Not!®

An arch is all that's left of an ancient Roman bridge over the Ludias River in Greece. The rest of the stones were looted by local farmers, who only stopped when they realized that everyone who had carried away stones . . .

a. died within a year.
b. lost all their teeth.
c. lost their farms.
d. became lepers.

Star Ship: In 1647, an English ship loaded with colonists disappeared. A year later, witnesses saw the ship appear in the sky over New England with astounding clarity. Henry Wadsworth Longfellow's poem, "The Phantom Ship," commemorates this event.

Possessed! The assassination of Archduke Franz Ferdinand of Austria started World War I. The car he was assassinated in is now in a Vienna museum. But before it was taken off the road, it was in *nine* accidents.

Believe It or Not!®

One night, the four Harner sisters, who slept in four separate bedrooms, were instantly killed by the same . . .

a. meteorite.
b. .38 caliber bullet.
c. firecracker.
d. bolt of lightning.

Trunk-ated Engagement:

The schooner *Susan and Eliza* was wrecked in a storm off Cape Ann, Massachusetts. Aboard was one of the shipowner's daughters, Susan Hichborn, who was on her way to her wedding in Boston. All 33 passengers perished. The only trace of the ship ever found was a trunk bearing Hichborn's initials and containing her possessions. It was cast ashore at the feet of her waiting fiancé.

That Sinking Feeling:

A Mississippi riverboat called the *Jo Daviess* sank after only three trips. Its engines were removed and installed on the steamboat *Reindeer,* and it sank, too. Salvaged once again, the engines were installed on the *Reindeer II,* which sank almost immediately. The engines were then used on the *Colonel Clay,* which sank after two trips. Next, the engines were installed on the S.S. *Monroe.* It was destroyed by fire. Salvaged for the fifth time, the engines were used in a gristmill, which burned to the ground.

Car Trouble: On his way to Salinas, California, movie star James Dean was driving 80 miles per hour when he was killed in a head-on collision. Investigators were puzzled by evidence that suggested that Dean, who was an expert driver, had done nothing to avoid the crash. Fans who flocked to the grisly scene were injured as they tried to remove pieces of the wreckage.

A garage mechanic, hired to restore the sports car, broke both legs when it fell on him. Two doctors bought parts from the car to reuse in their own race cars. After the parts were installed, one doctor died and the other suffered serious injury. The two undamaged tires were sold to a man who had to be hospitalized after they both blew out at the same time.

The California Highway Patrol planned to use the remains of the car in an auto show, but the night before the show opened, a fire broke out, destroying every vehicle but Dean's car, which escaped unscathed. The car was once again bound for Salinas when the driver lost control of the truck that was carrying it.

The driver was killed instantly. Dean's car rolled off the truck. The next effort to display the car also ended in calamity when the car, which had been carefully welded back together, inexplicably broke into 11 pieces. The

Florida police arranged to take the car for a safety display. But after the pieces of the car were crated and loaded onto a truck, the car disappeared, never to be seen again.

Believe It or Not!®

Five motorcycle racers who were killed in crashes over a period of four years had at least one thing in common when they died. They all . . .

a. wore the same helmet.
b. drove the same motorcycle.
c. had the same license plate number.
d. were talking on their cell phones.

A Grave Curse: Because the ancient Egyptians believed that the spirits of the dead returned to their bodies, they mummified bodies and sealed them in tombs. To open a tomb was to offend the gods. Between 1900 and 1976, more than 30 people who studied Egyptian tombs came to an untimely end. Could their deaths be the result of an ancient curse on the life of whoever dared enter?

Tut Tut! Tutankhamen—Tut for short—was pharaoh, or king, of Egypt from 1361 to 1352 B.C. He is one of the best known pharaohs because his tomb and its contents remained intact for more than 3,000 years. Though robbers stripped most pharaohs' tombs, Tut's wasn't discovered until 1922. Inside were thousands of treasures, including a jewel-encrusted throne made of silver and gold, and three ornamented nested coffins. Tut's body lay in the innermost coffin, which was made of solid gold.

Tomb and Doom: Famous Egyptologist Professor James Breasted, who was present at the first opening of Tut's tomb, died of fever. Shortly after loading the plane with artifacts from Tut's tomb, crew members suffered injuries.

Mummy Ship: The ocean liner *Titanic* was thought to be unsinkable. Could its sad fate have had something to do with its cargo, which included 2,200 passengers, 40 tons of potatoes, 12,000 bottles of mineral water, 7,000 sacks of coffee, 35,000 eggs—and an Egyptian mummy? There's really no way to tell.

Grave Warning: The tomb of the Turkish conqueror Tamerlane (1336–1405) in Samarkand, East Uzbekistan, bore an inscription that read, "If I should be brought back to Earth, the greatest of all wars will engulf this land." Soviet scientists, interested in studying historical burial practices, opened the tomb on June 22, 1941, at 5:00 A.M. and removed Tamerlane's mummified body. At the same moment, World War II broke out in Samarkand.

Homing Instinct: The *Dora*, originally a whaler from Port Townsend, Washington, was converted into a steamer by the Alaska Steamship Lines. In 1907, she lost her anchor in Cold Bay, Alaska, drifted without a compass for 92 days, and ended up at her old homeport in Washington. When the ship was taken out of the water, it was found that her hull had been badly damaged, and that the ship had been kept afloat by a rock wedged in the gaping hole.

Hands Off: In 1884, Walter Ingram returned to England, with the mummified hand of an ancient Egyptian princess. Clutched in the hand was a gold plaque that read, "Whoever takes me to a foreign land will die a violent death and his bones will never be found!" Four years later, Ingram was trampled to death by an elephant in Somaliland. He was buried in a dry riverbed, but when an expedition was sent to bring Ingram's body back to England, they discovered that it had been washed away by a flood.

Believe It or Not!®

A Gloucester schooner, wrecked and abandoned by its crew, blew a shrieking blast on its foghorn before plunging to the bottom of the sea. Its story inspired Henry Wadsworth Longfellow to write the poem, "The Wreck of the . . .

a. Maine."
b. Hesperus."
c. Bounty."
d. Pequod."

Queen-in-the-Box:

The night before Queen Elizabeth I of England was to be buried, her casket mysteriously exploded. Though the coffin was destroyed, the queen's body was unharmed.

Not So Safe:

Blasi Hoffman, a rich miser of Borken, Germany, locked his money in a safe in his room every night and slept with the key under his pillow. The moment he died on the night of July 9, 1843, the safe door flew open.

Remote Control: In

World War I, a British observation plane on the western front flew in wide circles for several hours and then landed without mishap—even though its pilot and observer were both dead.

Believe It or Not!®

Thirty years after killing a man on the island of Malta, sculptor Melchiore Caffa (1631–1687) felt so guilty that he created a statue of his victim to mark the grave. While putting the final touches on the sculpture . . .

a. the ghost of Caffa's victim appeared.
b. it toppled over, crushing Caffa to death.
c. it disintegrated.
d. Caffa was murdered.

You are entering a world of facts too bizarre to believe. You'll Believe It!—or Not! Three of the Ripley's oddities below are totally true. One is fully fictitious. Can you spot the fiction?

a. Many people in the mountain towns of Nepal believe that wearing mismatched socks while attempting a difficult climb up a mountain is bad luck. It is considered disrespectful—an affront to the mountain and to the gods.
Believe It!   Not!

b. In 1991, an appeals court in New York State officially declared a house in Nyack, New York, to be haunted.
Believe It!   Not!

c. Many hotels in China don't label the fourth floor because the character for four in the Chinese written language is the same as the character for death.
Believe It!   Not!

d. A poplar, planted in Jena, Germany, in 1815, to celebrate the end of the Napoleonic War with France, toppled suddenly 99 years later on August 1, 1914, the start of World War I.
Believe It!   Not!

BONUS QUESTION

The eye of the ancient Egyptian god Horus was a symbol of protection and healing. What contemporary symbol is derived from it?

a. The sign Rx used by physicians on prescriptions.

b. The @ symbol used in e-mail addresses.

c. The peace symbol.

Nearly a dozen ghosts have haunted the White House, many of them former presidents. Among those who have admitted to seeing these ghosts are Mary Todd Lincoln, Harry Truman, and William Howard Taft.

Ghostly Image: Of course there's no such thing as a ghost . . . but then who is that standing behind Mary Todd Lincoln in this photo taken many years after Abraham Lincoln's death? Is it Lincoln's ghost? An optical illusion? A fake?

Believe It or Not!®

Even though no one is there, family members often hear children running and laughing on the third floor of the Custis-Lee Mansion, which was once lived in by . . .

a. Bruce Lee.
b. Light-Horse Harry Lee.
c. Gypsy Rose Lee.
d. Robert E. Lee.

Haunted Hallways: Before he died, Abraham Lincoln told several people of a dream he'd had. In the dream, Lincoln saw a coffin lying in state in the East Room. When he asked who had died, he was told, "The president. He's been assassinated." Not long afterward, President Lincoln was murdered by an assassin's bullet. Since then, many people who have worked in the White House have reported seeing Lincoln's ghost roaming the hallways.

Jolly Spirit: When Andrew Jackson was president, his bedroom was in what is now called the Rose Room. After President Jackson died, deep laughter was heard coming from his room. Those who worked in the White House during his term of office recognized Jackson's laugh. The laugh has been heard at least once every four years ever since.

Ghostly Hijinks:

The students at Burnley School of Professional Art in Seattle, Washington, have grown accustomed to seeing some unusual sights—desks that appear to be moving

under their own steam, locked doors that open mysteriously by themselves, the sound of footsteps on vacant staircases. Who could be responsible? Could it be the ghosts of students past?

Believe It or Not!®

What English landmark is said to be haunted by the ghosts of Sir Walter Raleigh and Anne Boleyn?

a. Buckingham Palace
b. Westminster Abbey
c. Windsor Castle
d. The Tower of London

Spirited Uproars:

She was beheaded by her husband, King Henry VIII, so why do the servants at Hampton Court in England swear that Catherine Howard still roams the castle? It must be the bloodcurdling screams that come from her old rooms.

Friendly Phantom: It's a good thing that Christoph Gluck, a German composer who lived during the 1700s, believed in ghosts. Gluck got spooked after seeing an apparition of himself enter his bedroom and refused to sleep there that night. The next morning, Gluck discovered that the bedroom ceiling had collapsed over his bed and would have killed him had he slept there.

Sleepless in Zurich: For 900 years, no one has been able to stay overnight at a Hapsburg castle near Zurich, Switzerland. Why? Because the ghost of a murdered woman still screams in terror each and every

night without fail. As recently as 1978, one unbeliever, Horst Von Roth, who tried to stay the night, fled the haunted dwelling in horror.

Beatlemania? The members of the world-famous rock group the Beatles felt that they were able to speak to and receive messages from their manager, Brian Epstein—even after he had died.

Angelic Apparitions:

When the Wilcoxes' car broke down in New Mexico in 1966, a Mexican family whose surname was Angel offered them food and shelter. A year later, Mr. Wilcox stopped by to say hello, but to his surprise, a different family was living in the house, and no one had ever heard of the Angel family.

The Ghost at the Top of the Stairs:

During the 1970s, actor Richard Harris was constantly awakened at 2:00 A.M. by the banging of closet doors and the sound of little feet running up and down the tower stairs of his home. Only after he built a nursery at the top of the stairs and filled it with toys did the ghost become better behaved. The actor says he knew the ghost was a child because old records revealed that an eight-year-old boy was buried in the tower.

Believe It or Not!®

In the 1750s, Nellie Macquillie was drowned in a pool in North Carolina. Her ghost is still seen nearby, carrying her head under her arm. She's known as . . .

a. Headless Nellie.
b. No Noggin Nellie.
c. the Pool Ghoul.
d. the Headless Mermaid.

Riches from Witches: Johannesburg Castle in Aschaffenburg, Germany, was constructed between 1607 and 1614. It was paid for entirely with funds confiscated from women who were convicted of witchcraft.

Believe It or Not!®

If you live in Phoenix, Arizona, and your ancestors were witches, you might want to join an organization called . . .

a. Wicked Men of the West.
b. Broom Brood.
c. Sorcerer's Apprentices.
d. Sons of Witches.

Eyewitness: The Witch's Eye, near Thann, France, was used for years as a prison for persons accused of witchcraft. It is the only part of Englesbourg Castle that is still standing.

Witch Hysteria: In 1692, several young girls claimed they were being tormented by witches. As a result, 19 people in Salem, Massachusetts, were arrested, convicted of witchcraft, and hanged. One man, who refused to stand trial, was crushed to death.

Witch, Be Gone: Glass balls manufactured in the United States in the 19th century were hung in the windows of homes to ward off the evil spells of witches.

Probing Examinations: Sixteenth-century European witch-hunters used sharp probes to search victims for "the devil's mark"—skin areas such as a healed scar that did not bleed.

Burning Crusade:

Mathew Hopkins was the "witch-finder general" in 17th-century England, traveling around the country on his horrible missions. He determined guilt by throwing a suspected witch into a well. If the person floated, he or she was a witch and had to be burned at the stake.

Believe It or Not!®

In 1474, in the city of Basel, Switzerland, an animal was tried and found guilty of witchcraft. Was it a . . .

a. rooster for laying an egg?
b. hen for crowing cock-a-doodle-doo?
c. dog for not barking at intruders?
d. cow for not giving milk?

That Shrinking Feeling

No one knows how Robert Ripley learned the method used for shrinking heads from the Jivaro headhunters, since the practice had always been a closely guarded tribal secret.

Head Count: If two heads are better than one, Ripley must have been head and shoulders above the rest! These are just a few of the shrunken heads in Ripley's extensive collection.

Skullduggery

Certain cultures don't bury every skull with its body. Some skulls are saved to be used in ceremonial rituals.

Human Ram-ification: In Tibet, jeweled and silver-plated rams' heads are used in ceremonial rituals. Before 1949, they were fashioned from human skulls.

All Dressed Up and No Place to Go: Among Robert Ripley's souvenirs is a trophy New Guinea skull and a pig's tooth necklace.

Final Facial: Ancestor skulls from New Guinea were covered with clay.

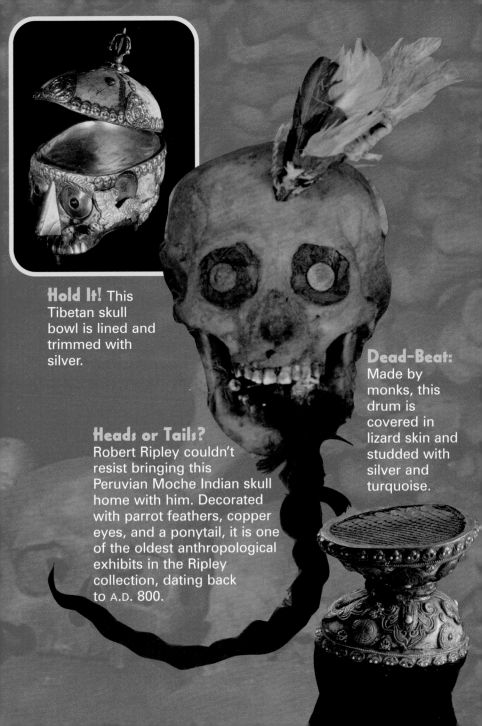

Hold It! This Tibetan skull bowl is lined and trimmed with silver.

Dead-Beat: Made by monks, this drum is covered in lizard skin and studded with silver and turquoise.

Heads or Tails? Robert Ripley couldn't resist bringing this Peruvian Moche Indian skull home with him. Decorated with parrot feathers, copper eyes, and a ponytail, it is one of the oldest anthropological exhibits in the Ripley collection, dating back to A.D. 800.

GRAVEYARD ARTS...

Dem Bones: For some, bones are the best things for . . .

making flutes

and beads . . .

or for decorating a church.

...and **CREEPY** CRAFTS

Cadaver Art: This horse and rider were created by Honoré Fragonard, who raided graveyards to find the perfect materials to create his masterpieces.

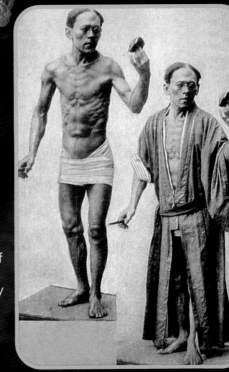

Body Double:
A sculptor named Masakitchi carved an exact replica of himself, complete with his own body hair, eyebrows, eyelashes, and nails.

ARE YOU MY

The ancient Egyptians believed that you *could* take it with you. Everything needed to have a fine time in the afterlife was buried with them.

Stuffed Animals: In ancient Egypt, cats were considered sacred. Some were mummified and buried with their owners, but cats also had their own tombs and burial grounds.

Tut's Guts: During the process of mummification, body organs were placed in canopic jars. The lids of these jars were fashioned to represent different gods.

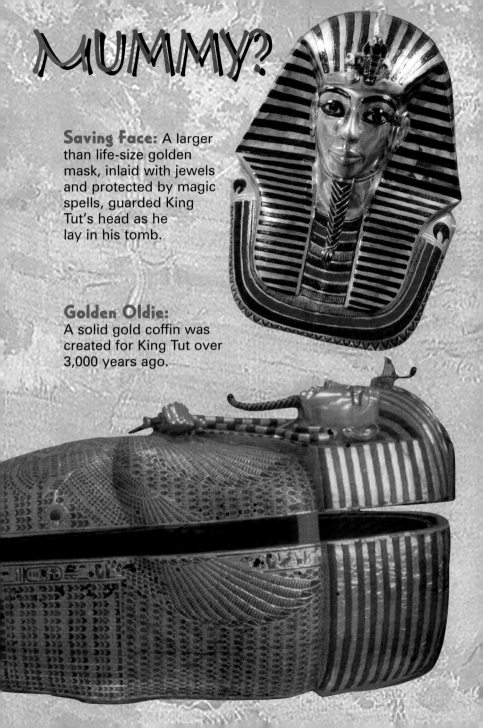

MUMMY?

Saving Face: A larger than life-size golden mask, inlaid with jewels and protected by magic spells, guarded King Tut's head as he lay in his tomb.

Golden Oldie: A solid gold coffin was created for King Tut over 3,000 years ago.

Playful Dead

For some, death is an opportunity to celebrate life . . .

Funky Fiesta: In Mexico, it is said, "We are not here for a long time—we are here for a good time." The Day of the Dead is one of the happiest days of the year, celebrated with puppets, masks, skull candies, and skeletons, of course.

Waking the Dead: In Madagascar, on the holiday Famadihana, loved ones are removed from their tombs, filled in on family gossip, and danced with before they are returned to their graves.

 **Brain Buster**

You know the drill. Go for it!

a. In 1574, Margaret Erskine of Dryburgh, Scotland, died suddenly and was buried in the family mausoleum. That night, when the sexton (the person who takes care of church property) tried to steal a ring from her finger, the dead woman sat up in her coffin and screamed. She lived for another 51 years!

Believe It!   **Not!**

b. Peter III of Russia was murdered in 1762 when he was 34 years old. He was crowned Emperor of Russia 34 years after his death—his coffin had to be opened so the crown could be placed on his head!

Believe It!   **Not!**

c. In 1985, Eric Villet of Orléans, France, was declared officially dead after doctors failed to revive him with heart massage and oxygen. He started breathing on his own three days later while lying in the morgue!

Believe It!   **Not!**

d. On May 16, 1997, William A. Hershorn was cutting through the cemetery on his way home. He tripped over a newly placed tombstone with the name W.A. Hershorn engraved on it along with the date of death, 5/16/97. Panicked, William ran out of the cemetery and into the street—where he was struck and killed by a car.

Believe It!   **Not!**

BONUS QUESTION

The White River Monster Sanctuary in Newport, Arkansas, was created by the state legislature for what purpose?

a. To make it illegal to vandalize a statue of a sea monster believed to have healing powers.

b. To make it illegal to "molest, kill, or trample" a legendary sea monster.

c. To make it illegal to kill or harm a Gila monster, a large black-and-orange venomous lizard that populates the area.

Some real-life stories are wilder than the tallest tales dreamed up by the most imaginative writers of fiction.

Queen of Denial: After the death of her husband, Prince Albert, in 1861, England's Queen Victoria continued to have his formal evening clothes laid out every day at Windsor Castle for the next 40 years.

Believe It or Not!®

On display at the Museum of the History of Science in Florence, Italy, is Galileo's . . .

a. first telescope.
b. middle finger.
c. notebook.
d. skull.

Cool Reception: Imelda Marcos threw a party in honor of her late husband's 73rd birthday. The former president of the Philippines attended, but was not very good company since he arrived frozen in his casket.

Head Trip: The secret of head-shrinking had always been fiercely guarded until Robert Ripley somehow got hold of it. This is what he found out about the process. First, the victim's head was removed. Then the scalp was slit down the middle, and the skull was pulled through the opening. Next, the lips were sewn up and hot stones and sand were poured into the cavity. Finally, the head was sewn shut and boiled in herbs until it had shrunk to the

size of a fist. The Jivaros of the Amazon forest in South America believed that to possess a warrior's head was to keep for oneself all the powers of the original owner.

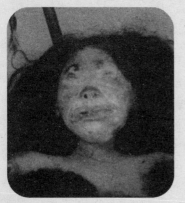

Ghoulish Figure: The Jivaros did not typically shrink female heads. However, the upper bodies of women were often prepared in the early 19th century to sell to tourists.

Saved by a Whisker: While on a ship at sea, the three-year-old Marquise de Maintenon was pronounced dead and sewn up in a sack to be thrown overboard. Luckily, her pet kitten had crawled inside the sack and began meowing during the funeral service. The mourners stopped the service, opened the sack, and discovered that the little girl was breathing. She later became the second wife of Louis XIV, and lived to the age of 84.

Babe in the Woods: Diego Quiroga, who was separated from his wife while fleeing Madrid during the French Invasion of 1811, found a newborn infant crying in a snow-covered field. He wrapped the baby in a blanket and carried her to the village of Venta de Pinar. There he learned the infant was his own daughter, born only a few hours earlier and abandoned by a nursemaid in the confusion of the flight.

Believe It or Not!®

Joseph Friedrich (1790– 1873) of Berlin, Germany, made an ivory miniature of the Church of St. Nicholas. The model developed a crack, and a few weeks later, the church did, too—in the same exact spot. Friedrich . . .

a. was publicly hanged.
b. lost his mind.
c. died of fright.
d. was struck by lightning.

Windows of the Soul:

Bedrooms in Grisons, Switzerland, have a tiny window that is opened only when the occupant is dying, to permit his or her soul to escape.

Mourning Pigeon:

A strange occurrence marked the burial service for Captain Joseph Belain, the man who had dedicated his life to saving the carrier pigeon from extinction. As if in tribute, a carrier pigeon flew in from the sea, perched on the bier, and stayed until the service was over.

Bumped Off: Countess Marie Arco of Austria found $50,000 in gold ducats in her garden, but never spent a single coin. Instead, she put the money in a chest and strapped it to the luggage rack inside her coach. She took the fortune everywhere she went until, on June 23, 1848, a bump in the road dislodged the treasure chest, which fell and killed her.

Three Times a Charm: In 1803, Joseph Samuels, sentenced to death by hanging for burglary in Hobart Town, Australia, was granted a reprieve by the governor after the rope broke three times.

Skullcap: In the Sainte Chapelle church in Paris, France, there is a bust of King Louis IX (1214–1270). What makes this sculpture so remarkable? A piece of the monarch's skull lies directly beneath the royal crown that sits on top of the sculpture's head.

Boning Up: Jeremy Bentham, who founded London's University Hospital in 1827, declared that no board meeting should ever take place without him. After his death in 1832, his cadaver was propped up at the conference table. Today, a wax replica sits in for Bentham, though his real head rests on the table. Of course, since Bentham cannot take an active part in the meetings, he is recorded as "present, but not voting."

Such a Headache: In 1867, William Thompson of Omaha, Nebraska, was shot by Native Americans of the Cheyenne tribe. Thinking he was dead, they removed his scalp. Imagine their surprise when Thompson regained consciousness, grabbed his scalp, and ran. He later donated the scalp to the Omaha Public Library.

"Bonified" Retreat: Six miles east of Prague in the Czech Republic, there is an 800-year-old chapel decorated entirely with bones. Bones are everywhere, giving the chapel a delicate, lacy appearance. A Czech woodcarver named Frantisek Rint bedecked the chapel with the bones of 40,000 people because, as the story goes, the nearby cemetery was filled, and many others were dying to be buried there.

Believe It or Not!®

One piece of cargo that traveled on the space shuttle *Discovery* in 1990 was a . . .

a. human skull.
b. monkey brain.
c. tadpole.
d. human eyeball.

Guilt Trip: In 1650, Oswald Kröl of Lindau, Germany, was convicted and executed for murder. Kröl was later vindicated. From that day on, his skeleton was propped up before the judge who had pronounced the death sentence.

Dead Ringer: Although he was well grounded in science, Thomas Edison was also interested in the psychic world. In fact, he invented (but never patented) a machine for communicating with the dead.

Believe It or Not!®

In Borneo, a human skull is placed between the bride and groom at weddings as a symbol . . .

a. of death, the penalty for infidelity.
b. that love can outlast death.
c. of ancestors watching over them.
d. that their children will outlive them.

Don't Leave Home Without It: Victorian vampire prevention kits had everything you'd need to survive a Transylvania vacation— a garlic necklace, a vial of holy water, a wooden stake, and a crucifix-shaped gun that fired silver bullets.

Tunnel Vision: The Tunnel of Posilipo in Naples, Italy, is 80 feet high, 22 feet wide, and $1/2$ mile long. It is completely illuminated by the sun only once each year— at sunset on Halloween.

Soulful Celebration: In Mexico, it is believed that the dead return once a year to visit with their loved ones. To make them feel welcome, relatives celebrate the Day of the Dead on the first two days in November, bedecking the graves with flowers and candles (*see color insert*).

Graveyard Bash: In Madagascar, an island off the coast of Africa, many people believe that honoring their dead loved ones with a sumptuous feast will bring the entire family good fortune. Every five years or so, families observe a holiday called Famadihana. The families remove their dead relatives from their tombs, tell them the most important family news, and even dance with them. Afterward, they give the bodies new shrouds and return them to their graves. (*See color insert.*)

Body of Work: In the 1700s, Honoré Fragonard, an anatomy teacher at a veterinary school, created bizarre objects out of animal and human cadavers. According

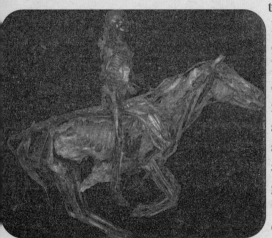

to Christophe Degueurce, curator of the Fragonard Museum, Fragonard obtained cadavers from veterinary schools, medical schools, executions, and even fresh graves. He stripped them of skin, dissected all the muscles and nerves, injected the blood vessels with wax, and steeped the bodies in alcohol for days. Finally, he stretched them into elaborate poses and dried them with hot air.

Ouch! When a woodcarver named Masakichi found out he was dying, he decided to leave a "living image" of himself to his beloved. After painstakingly plucking the hair from every pore in his body, he inserted each one in a corresponding position on a statue of himself he had carved. He included his eyebrows and eyelashes, then for the finishing touches, he pulled out his fingernails, toenails, and teeth, and attached them to his sculpture.

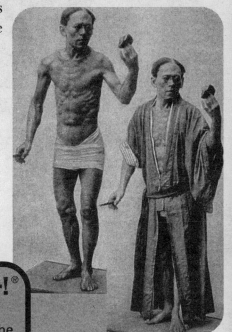

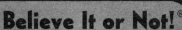
Believe It or Not!®

At Mount Minobu, Japan, Buddhists pay homage at the grave of Nichieren, founder of a Japanese sect, by . . .

a. allowing five candles on each outstretched arm to burn down to the flesh.
b. staying at the grave for two weeks without food or shelter.
c. walking on their knees to the gravesite.
d. holding their arms above their heads for an entire day.

Spin Cycle: The tombstone of Charles Merchant is a huge black granite sphere that has revolved on its stone pedestal once every year since it was built—despite the use of lead and cement to stop it.

Special Effects: A few years after the death of Smith Treadwell, an exact likeness of him appeared on his gravestone.

Believe It or Not!®

The grave of composer Wolfgang Amadeus Mozart in St. Marx Cemetery, Vienna, Austria, is noteworthy because . . .

a. the tomb is still unfinished.
b. it contains no body.
c. it's shaped like a flute.
d. it's shaped like a harpsichord.

Dead Bolt: Lightning shattered the tombstone of T.G. Brownell, who was killed by a bolt of lightning.

Miles to Go: In 1969, Miles Lucas of New Jersey was thrown from his car after it crashed into the wall of a cemetery. Lucas walked away from the accident, but his car kept going. It didn't stop until it finally landed on a headstone. The name of the headstone was Miles Lucas—no relation.

Lead Foot: Jonathan Blake's epitaph is a cautionary tale for speeders. It reads: Here lies the body of Jonathan Blake/Stepped on the gas instead of the brake.

Last Act: In a strange and bizarre twist of fate Ripley himself would have appreciated, he collapsed in 1949 while making the 13th episode of his live weekly television series. The segment was a dramatized sequence on the origin of "Taps"—a hauntingly sad tune played at military funerals. Ripley died two days later and was buried in his hometown of Santa Rosa, California, in a place called Oddfellows Cemetery.

Believe It or Not!®

The Ripley Memorial, which was in a church in Santa Rosa, California, was made out of . . .

a. a two-ton slab of granite.
b. eight million matchsticks.
c. a single giant redwood tree.
d. five thousand roses, which are replaced every week.

Straight from the crazy, mixed-up files of Mr. Robert L. Ripley, here are four facts that are just plain weird. Only catch is—one of them is totally made up. Can you figure out which one?

a. When Helen Jensen was a child, she swallowed a needle. Ouch! Thirty years later she found it in the thigh of her newborn baby.

Believe It!   **Not!**

b. A boy went to the doctor for a sore foot and found that a tooth was growing in his instep!

Believe It!   **Not!**

c. Brett Martin went to the doctor complaining of a severe earache only to find out that a pair of cockroaches was living in his inner ear.

Believe It!   **Not!**

d. A man came out of the hospital after recovering from a stroke and suddenly began speaking with a Scandinavian accent.

Believe It!   **Not!**

The book containing the transcript of the 1828 trial in which William Corder was convicted of murder can be seen in Moyses Hall Museum in Bury Saint Edmunds, England. What's so special about this book?

a. The text is written in Corder's own blood.

b. The text is bound in Corder's own skin.

c. The text glows bright red each year on the anniversary of Corder's trial.

POP QUIZ

Don't even think about closing this book! The Ripley's Brain Busters are not over yet. How much Creepy Stuff has stuck in your brain? How much raw Ripley's knowledge have you gained? It's time to find out! Circle your answers and give yourself five points for each question you answer correctly.

1. Which of the following is *not* an example of the sixth sense known as ESP?
a. A woman who can predict the outcome of court trials
b. A young girl who has a vision about the death of her pet before it happens
c. A woman who can name the ingredients of any perfume she smells
d. A woman who can run her hands over a map and point to places where oil will be found

2. Animals have amazing "sixth senses" of their own. After a man was killed while crossing the railroad tracks, Harry Goodman's dog would howl with fear whenever they approached the scene of the accident—even though the dog had not been there when the accident took place!
Believe It!   **Not!**

3. Which of the following is *not* believed by followers of astrology to affect the outcome of a person's life ?

a. The full moon.

b. The time, day, and month a person was born.

c. The position of furniture and other possessions in a room.

4. Which of the following strange coincidences is *not* true?

a. The Ebbins brothers from Bermuda died one year apart after being hit by the same taxicab driven by the same driver, carrying the same passenger.

b. George McDaniels and his father, mother, sister, two brothers, and an uncle all have the same birthday.

c. Kathy Moriarty and her seven sisters all had identical birthmarks in the exact same spot. Each sister has a crescent-shaped mole in the middle of her left cheek.

5. In the early 1900s, Harvey Lake, a conductor on a New Jersey train, made a big impression on the artistic director of the Academy of Music when he sang out the destinations in a beautiful tenor voice. The director immediately offered Lake a job as the star tenor in the New York City Opera.

Believe It!　　　　Not!

6. Which of the following is *not* a link between Abraham Lincoln and John F. Kennedy?

a. They were both shot on a Friday.

b. Each one's wife was present when he was shot.

c. They were both shot in a theater.

7. Which of the following objects is *not* believed to be cursed?
a. The Hope Diamond
b. The automobile in which James Dean died
c. The car in which John F. Kennedy was assassinated
d. The tomb of Tutankhamen, who was the pharaoh of Egypt from 1361 to 1352 B.C.

8. The ancient Egyptians believed that a person's spirit returned to his or her body after death. They also believed that to open a tomb was to offend the gods and bring a curse upon oneself.

Believe It!   Not!

9. Henry Wadsworth Longfellow's poem, *"The Phantom Ship,"* is about . . .
a. a ship that disappeared in 1647 and appeared as a vision in the sky a year later.
b. the *Titanic,* which was carrying an ancient Egyptian mummy when it sank.
c. a Mississippi riverboat that sank after only three trips. Its engines were installed in four other ships. Three sank, and one was destroyed by fire.

10. Which of the following is *not* a place where ghosts have been spotted according to the records of Robert Ripley?
a. The White House
b. The elementary school attended by former President Bill Clinton
c. The Tower of London
d. The Burnley School of Professional Art in Seattle, Washington

11. Which of the following former U.S. presidents is *not* believed by some to still haunt the White House?
a. Abraham Lincoln
b. Andrew Jackson
c. Richard M. Nixon

12. Three unrelated men named Charles Fairwell were the only survivors of three different airplane crashes in 1942, 1964, and 1985.
Believe It!   **Not!**

13. The Jivaro headhunters of the Amazon often shrunk the heads of men. Women escaped being victims—at least until the early 1900s, when the upper bodies of women were often prepared for sale to tourists.
Believe It!   **Not!**

14. Which of the following is *not* used to predict the future?
a. Chiromancy
b. Astrology
c. Numerology
d. Paleontology

15. The bust of King Louis IX in the Sainte Chapelle church in Paris, France, is amazing because . . .
a. the nose on the bust is Louis's actual preserved nose.
b. a piece of Louis's skull lies beneath the crown on the sculpture's head.
c. strands of Louis's hair, eyelashes, and eyebrows are affixed to the sculpture.

Answer Key

Chapter 1

Believe It or Not!

Page 5:   **a.** precognition.

Page 7:   **d.** extrasensory perception.

Page 9:   **c.** Lyndon B. Johnson

Page 11:   **c.** Nostradamus.

Page 13:   **b.** the moon is full.

Page 15:   **b.** his own death from natural causes.

Page 17:   **c.** Theodore Roosevelt.

Page 19:   **c.** In India.

Page 20:   **b.** it snowed three times.

Brain Buster: a. is false.

Bonus Question: c.

Chapter 2

Believe It or Not!

Page 23:   **d.** George Washington.

Page 24:   **a.** pants zipper.

Page 27:   **a.** Gemini.

Page 29:   **b.** Harry S Truman.

Page 31:   **a.** 13th floor.

Page 33:   **c.** by another Claude Volbonne who was unrelated to his father's murderer.

Page 34:   **b.** Bermuda Triangle.

Brain Buster: b. is false.

Bonus Question: b.

Chapter 3

Believe It or Not!

Page 37:   **a.** died within a year.

Page 38:   **d.** bolt of lightning.

Page 41:   **a.** wore the same helmet.

Page 43:   **d.** mummies.

Page 45:   **b.** *Hesperus.*"

Page 46:   **b.** it toppled over, crushing
             Caffa to death.

Brain Buster: a. is false.

Bonus Question: a.

Chapter 4

Believe It or Not!

Page 49:   **d.** Robert E. Lee.

Page 51:   **d.** The Tower of London

Page 53:   **a.** Headless Nellie.

Page 54:   **d.** Sons of Witches.

Page 56:   **a.** rooster for laying an egg?

Brain Buster: d. is false.

Bonus Question: b.

Chapter 5

Believe It or Not!

Page 59:   **b.** middle finger.

Page 61:   **c.** died of fright.

Page 62:   **a.** the palm of their hand.

Page 65:   **a.** human skull.

Page 66:   **b.** that love can outlast death.

Page 69:   **a.** allowing five candles on each outstretched arm to burn down to the flesh.

Page 70:   **b.** it contains no body.

Page 72:   **c.** a single giant redwood tree.

Brain Buster: **c.** is false.

Bonus Question: b.

Pop Quiz

1. **c.**
2. **Believe It!**
3. **c.**
4. **c.**
5. **Not!**
6. **c.**
7. **c.**
8. **Believe It!**
9. **a.**
10. **b.**
11. **c.**
12. **Not!**
13. **Believe It!**
14. **d.**
15. **b.**

What's Your Ripley's Rank?

Ripley's Scorecard

Congrats! You've busted your brain on some crazy, creepy facts and challenged your ability to tell fact from fiction. Now it's time to rate your Ripley's knowledge. Are you a Spooky Superstar or a Ripley's Realist? Check out the answers in the answer key and use this page to keep track of how many trivia questions you've answered correctly. Then add 'em up and find out how you rate.

Here's the scoring breakdown—give yourself:
★ **10 points** for every **Believe It or Not!** you answered correctly;

★ **20 points** for every fiction you spotted in the **Ripley's Brain Busters**;

★ **10** for every **Bonus Question** you answered right;

★ and **5** for every **Pop Quiz** question you answered correctly.

Here's a tally sheet:
Number of **Believe It or Not!** _____ x 10 = _____
questions answered correctly:

Number of **Ripley's Brain Buster** _____ x 20 = _____
questions answered correctly:

Number of **Bonus Questions** _____ x 10 = _____
answered correctly:

Chapter Total: _____

Write your totals for each chapter and the Pop Quiz section in the spaces below. Then add them up to get your FINAL SCORE. Your FINAL SCORE decides how you rate:

Chapter One Total: _____

Chapter Two Total: _____

Chapter Three Total _____

Chapter Four Total: _____

Chapter Five Total: _____

Pop Quiz Total: _____

FINAL SCORE: _____

525-301
Spooky Superstar

You are eerily excellent. You've got a sixth sense for the spooky and a gripping grasp on the gory. Your Ripley's know-how is top-notch. Nothing creeps you out. And nothing gets past you—you can spot a fantasy-fact miles away! Your ability to tell fact from fiction is out of the ordinary and unbelievably amazing. You are a force to be reckoned with. Keep up the good work!

300-201
Amazing Ace

You are creeping your way up to the top of the ranks. You know a true tale when you see one—spooky or not. And your sense for the suspicious is supercharged. You're no sucker for a made-up ghost story or a tall tale, but you find yourself getting carried away once in a while. That's okay! Go with your gut—you've got superstar potential.

200-101
Creepy Convert

Your eye for the eerie is getting better. But the mere thought of the dead coming back to life or a ghost in the attic sends chills down your spine. You may not be totally gullible, but it's fairly easy to trick you with a phony fact or made-up mystery. If "seeing is believing," you tend to believe what you read. Keep working on your sixth sense—you'll be amazed by what you can do.

100-0
Ripley's Realist

You're a down-to-earth, believe-it-when-you-see-it kind of person. Sure, you may not pay enough attention to tales of ghosts, goblins, witches, or even superstitions to be able to spot the fiction among the facts, but you like it that way. And while you totally get that truth can be stranger than fiction, your no-nonsense attitude helps you deal with anything remotely out of the ordinary. Case closed.

Photo Credits

Ripley Entertainment Inc. and the editors of this book wish to thank the following photographers, agents, and other individuals for permission to use and reprint the following photographs in this book. Any photographs included in this book that are not acknowledged below are property of the Ripley Archives. Great effort has been made to obtain permission from the owners of all materials included in this book. Any errors that may have been made are unintentional and will gladly be corrected in future printings if notice is sent to Ripley Entertainment Inc., 5728 Major Boulevard, Orlando, Florida 32819.

Black & White Photos

6 Franklin D. Roosevelt; 19 King George III; 29 Lightning/CORBIS

6 Warren G. Harding; 9 William Blake; 20 Bust of Julius Caesar; 38 Archduke Ferdinand; 44 Tamerlane; 51 Catherine Howard/Bettmann/CORBIS

7 Jeanne Dixon/Associated Press UNIVERSAL PRESS SYNDICATE

9 General MacArthur and Troops; 26 Mark Newman and Jerry Levey; 52 Brian Epstein/Associated Press

11 Fire; 15 Oil Rig; 31 Apple/Copyright Ripley Entertainment and its licensors

13 Chris Robinson/Chris Robinson

20 *The Old Farmer's Almanac*/ www.almanac.com

25 Mel Gibson/Rogers & Cohen

31 Black Cat/Santokh Kochar/PhotoDisc

32 Abraham Lincoln/Library of Congress, Prints and Photographs Division, LC-USZ62-13016 DLC

6, 32 John F. Kennedy/Photo No. ST-C237-1-63 in the John F. Kennedy Library

34 Dalai Lama/Galen Rowell/CORBIS

34 Shipwreck/Mark Downey/PhotoDisc

37 Hope Diamond/Smithsonian Institution

43 Tutankhamen's Tomb/Hulton-Deutsch Collection Limited/CORBIS

49 Mary Todd Lincoln/The Lloyd Ostendorf Collection

50 Andrew Jackson/Library of Congress, Prints and Photographs Division, LC-USZ62-5099 DLC

54 Johannesburg Castle/Franziska Oelmann

63 Hangman's Rope/Laura Miller

64 Sainte Chapelle/The Paris Pages

65 Bone Church/Ben Fraser

68 Fragonard Sculpture/C. Degueurce

Color Insert

Canopic Jar/Richard Carr

Day of the Dead Candy Skulls; Day of the Dead Skeleton on Stilts/Ann Murdy

Famadihana/AP Photo/Toussaint Raharison

King Tut Sarcophagus/Roy Slovenko

If you enjoyed **Creepy Stuff**, you'll love

In this amazing album of the most incredible individuals on Earth, you'll meet . . .

Shannon Pole Summers, the girl who can pull a pickup truck filled with her high school football team

Robert Wadlow, the tallest man of all time

Jean-Yves Blondeau, who skates on his elbows, hands, knees, and chest

Ignatz von Roll, a poultry farmer who outfitted his turkeys in Turkish turbans

These are just a small sampling of the weird and wacky characters in **Odd-inary People**. You'll be amazed at the things some people will do! **Believe It!**®